Enjoy!

Jean Daish

Operation Pied Piper

Jean Daish was born in Leeds and is the wife of a former Royal Air Force Officer. Along with son Andrew and daughter Susannah, the family became used to moving house throughout Great Britain and overseas. Cornwall was home for several years.

Inspired by the birth of her first of four grandchildren sixteen years ago, Jean attended a writing course and began writing short stories, articles and poetry for children. *Operation Pied Piper* is her first book.

Following twenty-seven house moves during their time with the RAF, Jean and her husband are now settled in Buckinghamshire.

Operation Pied Piper

Operation Pied Piper

Written and Illustrated by Jean Daish

Olympia Publishers
London

www.olympiapublishers.com
OLYMPIA PAPERBACK EDITION

A CIP catalogue record for this title is
available from the British Library.

ISBN: 978-1-84897-281 0

First Published in 2013

Olympia Publishers
60 Cannon Street
London
EC4N 6NP

Printed in Great Britain

Dedication

For Susannah

Acknowledgments

I would like to thank Margaret Nash, published children's author and 'SMARTIE' prize winner, for all the tuition, encouragement and friendship, which I have received over many years.

My thanks go also to my 'writing group' friends in Winslow.

Thanks to Kim Richardson for his wise council.

Thank you for my grandchildren, Patrick, Jonathan, Tilly and Theo – who are my inspiration and joy – and the rest of my family.

A great big thank you to my husband John, who has shown great patience during the book's development; I could not have written *Operation Pied Piper* without his practical and emotional support.

PROLOGUE

Evacuation means 'leaving a place'. During the Second World War, many children living in big cities and towns were moved, temporarily, from their homes to places considered safer, usually out in the countryside or by the sea. The British evacuation began on Friday 1st September 1939. It was called 'Operation Pied Piper'.

This is the story of a group of children evacuated to Cornwall. For some children evacuation was a big adventure, but for others, never having been away from home before, there would have been confusion and even fear. But there were friendships to be made also and many lasted, not just for the duration of the War, but for a lifetime.

The children in this story are fictional but 'Operation Pied Piper' was a real event.

CHAPTER 1

1st September 1939
The Departure

I stood on Leeds City Station platform with my gloved hand in Aunt Jean's, looking around at the hoards of children. Glum, tired, all shapes, sizes and ages clutching their pathetic cases, precious teddies and with their brown boxed gas masks hung over drooping shoulders. A sorry army of children being torn apart from their families. The younger ones not understanding. That was the worst part. We were evacuees being transported away from our homes to safety. Or so we were told. I slipped off my glove and felt the warmth of Auntie's hand over mine.

"It's Government policy love – for your own safety and it won't be forever – you'll see. You'll love the country and the sea Polly – you will. Much warmer than up here." Aunt Jean dabbed at her eyes, smiling unconvincingly. A quick peck on my cheek and I was gently ushered into a carriage. There was an overpowering smell of soot, dirt and fear.

"There, you can sit next to that little girl in the brown coat – she looks as if she could do with a friend."

There was an ear splitting whistle and a grinding and groaning of metal and the train slowly shunted forward. The platform filled with steam and I could just make out Aunt Jean waving her handkerchief. She was shouting something but it was impossible to hear her. I hadn't even said goodbye. I sank miserably into my seat as the train increased speed.

There were four of us in the carriage. Two scruffy little boys about seven and an older girl in a forlorn brown coat. There was a dank, dirty smell – probably one of the boys. I shuffled closer to the girl.

"Would you like to share my dinner?" I said, reaching into the brown paper bag and retrieving a potted meat sandwich. Without a word the sandwich was snatched from my fingers and plunged into the girl's mouth. I reached across and gave two to the boys.

"I feel sick," said the boy with a shock of blond curls.

"I'll 'ave it," said the other devouring one sandwich and shoving the other into his coat pocket.

Through the carriage door and down the corridor I could hear quiet chatter. There was some crying but also the sound of excited voices. For some of the children this was a big adventure. But as I sank deeper into the corner of the carriage, wrapping my coat closer around me, I just felt a sickening dread.

***

I woke up with the taste of salty potted meat in my mouth, feeling very thirsty. I reached into my paper bag for a small bottle of milk. The girl had moved to sit opposite me with the boys. She had her feet up on the seat – her shoes touching my coat. I saw the holes in the soles and one shoe had a lace missing. She stirred, yawned and scratched her head.

"Got any more of them sandwiches?"

"'Fraid not," I lied. "You can have the rest of my milk though."

Once again the grubby hand reached out and snatched the bottle without a word of thanks.

"'Ere you boys – 'ave a sip." Slurping down the remains of the milk, she wiped her mouth with the back of her hand then threw the bottle onto the floor where it rumbled under the seat.

"What's that name on your label then?" She peered at the label on my coat.

"Polly," I replied, reaching under the seat to retrieve the empty bottle.

"That's a funny name," she giggled.

"'Ow old are ya?"

"I'll be eleven in two days' time on 3rd September. You're Vera," I said scanning the label on the brown coat.

"I am that – named after me Mam. It's short for Veronica, I'm ten as well."

We sat in silence, gazing through grimy windows onto the backs of equally grimy houses.

"Was that your Mam then – that woman that saw ya off?"

"No, it was my Auntie Jean – my mother died last year. She was very ill." I felt a sudden rush of homesickness mingled with panic and, to my horror, tears filled my sore eyes and spilled over onto my lap.

"Sorry," said Vera clumsily. She sniffed loudly, placed her grubby shoes down on the floor and settled herself into the corner.

"Got any brothers and sisters then 'ave ya?"

My pretence at being asleep hadn't worked.

"No – there's just me – what about you?"

"Me brother's in the army – 'e's been away ages. Too bloomin' long Mam says. I can 'ear her crying at night sometimes. There's me Dad but Mam says 'e's worse than a man short. 'E's only got one leg, well two really but one's wooden."

I hid a smile.

The train suddenly lurched forward and one of the boys landed on my lap.

"Oooh look, Polly."

Vera leapt to her feet and pointed to the distant sea.

"Flippin' 'eck – that's grand, that is – never seen so much water outside Cookridge Baths."

I brushed my coat sleeve where one of the boys had wiped his nose.

"What's that about Cookridge Baths?"

"Me Mam, Dad and me – we all go to Cookridge Street Baths once a week for a hot bath. We're too big for the tin baths, you see."

"You mean you don't have a bathroom?"

"No – toffee nose – we don't 'ave a bathroom. And the lav's outside and it's freezing – and we use newspaper to wipe our bums. So there!!"

For the next few hours, except for stops at deserted country stations, the train rumbled on until we reached Plymouth.

After crossing the Brunel Bridge, which I knew was the bridge which joined Devon to Cornwall, the train increased speed as if it couldn't wait to despatch its cargo of desolate children on to Bodmin Moor.

Finally, the tired old iron horse drew into Bodmin Station. There was an immediate increase in noise and anxious faces were pressed to the windows. Struggling into coats and retrieving battered suitcases, we all waited for the next move. Would anyone be there on the platform to meet us? Where would we have to go? One of the boys snivelled.

"I wanna go 'ome to me Mam," he gulped.

"Well ya can't so shurrup," said his brother.

Vera put an arm around the boys.

"Don't worry love – we'll stick together." She wiped his nose with the hem of her blouse.

What on earth did she mean – 'we'll stick together?' I didn't want to stay another minute with this lot!

CHAPTER 2

There was chaos on the platform. Adults were patrolling, their flashlights piercing the gloom, as they separated the children into groups. As names were called the groups became more orderly, but subdued. We were a sorry sight – like bundles of clothing being sorted for the laundry, instead of sad little people, homesick and fearful. I had no idea where Vera and the boys were.

"Please can I hold your hand?" said a small girl at my side.

Two little girls, twins I think, stood beside me; I took a small, cold hand in mine.

"Where are we going?" said one. The other was whimpering.

"Padstow," I said. "I've got Quay Cottage on my instructions – let me see – yes – yours is the same. Where's your gas mask?" I asked one.

"I left it on the train."

"Don't move either of you – I'll go and get it."

One of the helpers was handing out supplies of spare gas masks. I grabbed one and returned to the girls.

"Come on – we have to board that coach – stay close and don't lose your gas mask again. Don't cry – I'm not cross – hurry!"

I found a seat behind the driver, threw my bag underneath and put the girls in the seat behind me.

"Try and have a sleep," I said to the one with her thumb firmly stuck in her mouth, her eyes drooping. "It could be a while before we get to Padstow."

Wrapping my coat around me, running my fingers through the condensation on the window, I tried to see through the murk what was happening outside. Over the cacophony of voices and hissing steam, I recognised Vera's raucous shout!

"Come on lads follow me – flippin' 'eck don't ya want to get to the seaside?"

I sank lower into my seat as Vera and the boys rushed past to the coach behind.

"Everyone OK?" shouted the driver. There were a few weary replies as the coach lurched forward and gathered speed as it left the chaos of the station and headed for Padstow. I woke with a jolt. The coach was steaming downhill jogging its passengers from their drugged sleep.

"Hold tight – we're here now – just heading for the quay."

Four tight little fists gripped the back of my seat as we came to a halt. It was pitch black outside the coach, but we could hear the wind and raging seas and it sounded very close.

"Come on girls, we're here – make sure you have everything," I encouraged them, trying to keep the anxiety out of my voice. The twins hung on to my coat as we huddled together waiting for more instructions.

"I'm cold," said one.

"Me too," said the other. I couldn't see their faces, but I felt their trembling.

***

We were guided through the gloom towards a cottage on the quay. A warm glow seeped through the crack in the front door but all the windows were blacked out. The driver banged on the door which was opened by a tiny, round lady. "Three for you, Mrs Trewithen," he said pushing us gently forward.

"Goodness me – you poor lambs. Come in this instant and close the door quickly after you – blackout regulations, but you know all about that don't 'ee."

A large man with flaming red hair, a red beard and a patch over one eye came forward. "This 'ere is Mr Trewithen girls, my husband, but you can call him Denzil. Everyone calls me Mother but you won't want to do that will 'ee my lovelies? Take their things upstairs Denzil while I get them something to eat."

Mrs Trewithen leant down and gently helped the little girls out of their coats, all the time cooing and comforting them, rubbing their freezing hands between her warm plump ones.

"Is the man a pirate?" asked one of the girls.

"Goodness no, my lovely – just a big soft old lad – so don't 'ee be afraid. Now for some hot soup and then bed."

We fell on our soup, exhausted and hungry.

"Right climb the stairs to Bedfordshire then Polly, and you two…"

"Nellie," replied one twin and "Rose," said the other.

My room was sparse. There was a three-quarter bed, a side table, small wardrobe and chest of drawers. The window almost touched the floor. At least I had a room to myself. I undressed quickly without washing, although there was a jug of water and a bowl on the table, and a chamber pot under the bed. I could hear the girls next door and through the window the sound of the angry sea. I climbed wearily into the bed, delighted to find a hot water bottle. I was comfortable but homesick, my stomach was leaden, my eyes burned with unshed tears. Be brave, Auntie had said. But how brave must I be and for how long?

CHAPTER 3

Our first breakfast at Quay Cottage was a cheery affair. Denzil had picked eggs off the nest for us and there was steaming porridge with a teaspoon of honey. The twins chatted and giggled, as if they had lived here forever, with no sign of homesickness. Our breakfast was disturbed by a loud knock on the cottage door and voices in the passage.

"Flippin' 'eck – it's toffee nose!" Vera launched herself into the kitchen followed by Denzil.

"Another for the brood Mother," said Denzil drawing Vera into the room. "This 'ere is Vera."

Mrs Trewithen dried her hands on her apron and put another bowl on the table. "Goodness me child, you look worn out. Sit down this instant and Denzil will fetch another egg."

"Where are the boys, Vera?" I asked, making more room around the table.

"What boys?" said Mrs Trewithen, filling Vera's bowl with steaming porridge.

"They travelled down to Cornwall with us – Vera and me, Mrs Trewithen." Vera slurped her porridge hungrily.

"Still up at the big house on the cliff, poor little beggars. There was a woman in a Fair Isle cardi – housekeeper in charge – 'orrible dragon." The spoon was licked clean and Vera sat back contentedly.

"Thanks lady – that was grand – starving I was."

"What about the dragon, Vera?" I prompted.

"Well she wanted slaves she did. She asked *me* if I could cook and I said a bit – she asked me if I could make a fire and I said 'no' – she asked me if I could fill a coal bucket and I said 'no'. I got this condition ya see Mrs, I said – makin' fires, fillin' coal buckets it would kill me!" The twins eyes widened in wonder at Vera. "Wiv that she sent me packing, to be rehoused she said, and 'ere I am. I'm a bit worried though about the lads Billy and Jack."

"And what *is* this condition you have young lady?" queried Mrs Trewithen.

"Oh there's nowt wrong wi' me – strong as a horse, Mrs. I wasna goin' to cook for that old dragon. Shall I wash up for ya, Mrs?"

And Vera rolled up her sleeves.

***

That first day in Padstow was spent mainly indoors. The storm of the previous day was still blowing itself out. Vera helped Mrs Trewithen with the washing we girls had produced and the kitchen filled with the steaming warm smell as it dried on the airers around the fire-cum-cooker, while I amused the twins with stories of

Auntie's sweet shop. Dear Auntie, how I missed her. I wondered, was she missing me?

***

Vera and I were to share a bedroom. I was embarrassed, never having shared a room before, but lost all thoughts of shyness when, out of the corner of my eye, I saw Vera pull her jumper over her head and standing only in voluminous knickers and vest, she jumped into bed pulling the sheet up to her grinning face.

"Flippin' 'eck we got a hottie, Poll!"

I slid into the narrow bed trying not to touch Vera. "Come on Poll, cuddle up, it'll keep us warm." She leant into me, her bony shoulder digging into mine. "You never shared affore, Poll?"

"No, never."

"I 'ad to sleep with me Mam, Polly." I turned my back on Vera and tried to disappear into the pillow and fell asleep to the sound of Vera's gentle snoring.

CHAPTER 4

"'Appy birthday Toffee Nose."

Vera kneeling on the bed started to sing. The girls next door joined the bedlam and I struggled to wake up. "How ever did you know, Vera?"

"Ya said on't train that first day. You're eleven today Poll. I aint got a card for ya but ya can 'ave a kiss." And a wet mouth was pressed firmly to my cheek.

"Me next, me next." And so first Nellie then Rose hugged and kissed me and I rewarded them with tears.

"I'm sorry, it's just… It's just I miss Auntie and the shop and Trouble the cat and there won't be a card because Auntie doesn't know where I am yet."

"Don't cry Polly – it's your birthday," said the twins giving me a second hug. "Let's go for breakfast, I'm starving." Vera plucked at my nightgown.

The kitchen was empty. There was no breakfast on the table and the kitchen door stood wide open. "Where is everybody?" said Vera.

 The radio was on and we caught the tail end of a news bulletin. Something about a declaration. Denzil's large frame filled the doorway into the kitchen and he walked over to the radio and switched it off.

"My dears, sit down and listen carefully." Denzil looked sombre. The twins sat, huge eyed, holding each other's hands and Vera and I sat in silence.

"We've declared war, girls. We are now at war with Germany. It was expected but it is still a shock and a terrible thing but you are quite safe 'ere – Mother and I will take care of you until it's all ended and you can go 'ome again. You can tell your folks that all is well, to put their minds at rest like. Now Vera, put the kettle on and we'll all 'ave a cuppa sweet tea. Mrs M is just next door with a neighbour – 'er lad might be goin' to France."

"Oh Poll," Vera clasped my hand in hers. "Fancy declaring war on your birthday!"

"What's that about a birthday?" Denzil, his red beard quivering was dabbing at his good eye with a spotted handkerchief.

"It's Polly's birthday today, Denzil. Can we make a cake?" Nellie jumped up and down excitedly.

"I think that's a splendid idea young Nellie, you go and see if them 'ens 'ave got anything for us today. We can't let Polly miss out on a birthday treat, war or no." And so Nellie went to collect the precious eggs off the nests whilst I laid the table for breakfast.

Vera stood looking out of the window, her whole frame slumped. She was crying. "Vera, Vera what is it?" I put my arms around her thin shoulder and felt the weight of sorrow.

"Whatever is goin' to 'appen to my brother Poll, and – and Mam – 'ow is she goin' to manage on 'er own without 'im and me?"

"But your father is still with her Vera – he'll take care of her surely?" Vera's tear stained face turned to mine told me otherwise.

"Come on Vera, let's make a cake. It will cheer everyone up," I said. And it did.

CHAPTER 5

Sitting on the edge of my bed, I looked on to the quay below and the mud flats left behind by the receding tide. The early sun bounced off the boat decks and, here and there, a spinnaker rattled. But above it all, the sound of swooping, crying seagulls, scavenging yesterday's dropped fish and chips.

"What you thinkin' about Poll?" Vera asked struggling into her voluminous knickers.

"I was thinking of home, Vera, and how much Auntie would love Padstow. She really needs a holiday."

Vera came and sat on the bed, putting her arms around my shoulder. I found it surprisingly comforting.

"Where's your Dad, Poll – you never said?"

"Dad was a fireman – full time. He loved it. He died two years before Mum. There was an accident."

"What kind of accident?" asked Vera.

"A little boy had fallen into the River Aire near Leeds Bridge. Dad's fire-crew was putting out a factory fire nearby. Dad was called to the bridge – dived in – brought the boy to the surface. But someone said there was another child in the water. Dad dived in time and time again, but then – he didn't come up. It was a hoax –

you know – pretend. Anyway, he drowned – Dad. Mum never recovered and she died two years later."

"Well I never," Vera whispered. "I know my dad's useless but at least he's *there* – good leg restin' on the fire grate – you poor thing, Polly."

Vera put her arm around me once more. She really was very sweet, but I could feel the tears well up and I pulled away gently. "Come on, Vera – let's see what jobs Ma wants us to do today."

As usual Denzil was stirring the porridge, his massive frame taking up far too much space in the kitchen. Nellie and Rose sat cute as buttons at the table. We knew nothing about the twins, and the boys all by themselves at the Gull House. What were they up to?

"Can we do some shopping Ma or tidying?" Vera asked.

"I think you should all spend some time this morning writing to your parents and then take them to the Post Office on the quay. P'raphs you can help the little uns, Polly – make sure their spelling's right," said Ma.

With a little encouragement the twins and Vera finished their letters home. The twins knew their address – near Leeds Town Hall and Vera, shielding her letter with her arm – well, I'm not sure where she lived. I didn't care. We had become friends and *that* was the most important thing.

35

"Polly, I trust you to take care of the twins, hold their hands and you Vera can carry the basket. After you've posted the letters, buy three slices of ham – we'll manage to make that do for all of us. Watch the purse Vera."

We headed off to the village shop-cum-Post Office, our spirits lifted by the early sun. The twins broke away from me and skipped along ahead. They didn't seem at all homesick.

We had just come out of the shop when we collided into two boys. It was Billy and Jack, snotty nosed as ever. Jack had a nasty bruise on his cheek. I leant down and gently traced it with my finger.

"Boys, we were wondering what had happened to you," I said.

"Not supposed to talk to anybody," said Billy sullenly.

"We'll get into bother," whispered Jack.

I grabbed two hands and pulled them round to the back

of the shop. Vera and the twins stood wide eyed.

"What do you mean – can't talk to anybody? Why not?"

"She said – 'er – Mrs Tremaine the housekeeper – said we should keep our mouths zipped about anything we saw or 'eard – didn't she, our Billy? Except we ain't seen or 'eard anythin' – too much work to do."

"Except the ghost!" piped up Billy.

"Don't be daft," Vera laughed.

"What ghost, Billy?" I asked.

"It's the phantom pirate – it is. You can 'ear 'im at night draggin' 'is peg leg across the floor up above – not loud – just sort of clickin' and draggin'."

"'As she told ya that rubbish – Mrs Tremaine?" Vera scoffed.

"Yes Vera. But ya mustn't say a word – else 'e'll come an' slit our throats from ear to ear."

Vera wiped Billy's nose with her sleeve. "The 'orse faced old bat. Why ever did they take ya in?"

"They won't take any more in since you left, Vera," Billy sniffed.

"We'll sort things out won't we, Polly? We'll make sure you're alright lads," said Vera.

I wasn't sure what exactly we were going to do to help, but I agreed with Vera. We guessed who had made that bruise on Billy's face.

"Go back, pretend you haven't seen anyone, boys, and what were you doing here anyway?" I asked Jack.

"Getting some bread and cheese. Mrs Binns – she cooks – she's poorly today so we're doin' the shoppin'. That's right isn't it, Billy? We've only had bread and cheese since we went up to Gull House."

And judging by the smell of their clothes, they hadn't had much in the way of a wash either.

The boys waved wanly as they walked off. It was hard, letting them go. Something really had to be done to help them.

CHAPTER 6

The letter

I felt Vera tossing and turning beside me in her sleep that night. She said we should do something to help Billy and Jack, but what? I thought we should tell Denzil, especially about the bruise on Jack's poor face.

"Vera, Polly, girls, breakfast!" Ma shouted up the stairs.

"Something for you Polly – something special I shouldn't wonder." Beaming broadly Mrs M put a bulky envelope on my plate.

The twins bounced up and down with glee, shaking the table.

"It's your birthday card, Vera, from your Auntie – let's see, let's see."

"I think I will open it later twins, after breakfast." I'm sure they didn't understand. Their little faces crumpled. But I wanted to open it all by myself. I looked across at Vera. There was no letter for her – not yet. She sniffed loudly – she always did that when she was anxious – but she smiled at me.

"If it's a bag of sweets – we'll 'ave one – won't we, twins?" And Vera started on her porridge.

My dear Polly,

Your birthday card is a bit late but better late than never, I say.

Just seeing Auntie's writing made my tummy turn somersaults. The card had a fat black cat on the front. Auntie would know how much I was missing Trouble.

You sound very comfortable with Mr and Mrs Trewithen, and your new friends sound nice. What a lot of work for Mrs Trewithen. I do hope you all help out.

Things have changed quite a lot dear, since you left. We've had to put tape all over the windows – crisscross – just in case there should be air raids. And we have what's called blackout curtains and blinds to make sure no lights show outside the houses. Is it the same in Cornwall, I wonder? You didn't say. But there's no sign of nonsense yet from the blessed Jerries.

Our Trouble has taken to sleeping on the end of my bed. I think he misses you. He's so fat and heavy though he makes my feet go numb! It's nice to have his company though. We've had practice Air Raid sirens and he doesn't like those, hides under the sofa in the kitchen poor thing.

You sound very well dear. No coughs and colds now you are living by the sea. I knew you would like it. Don't forget us though, will you Polly?

Poor Mr Krantz – you know the gentleman with the shoe mending shop. He had his windows broken yesterday. Ignorant little devils down the street at No. 8. I know he's German but he's lived in Leeds since he was six. He can't very well go back to Germany – he has no-one there poor man.

There's talk of food rationing after Christmas, so we will only be able to buy so much butter and things for the week. I'm not sure how the sweets will go. Maybe no-one will be able to buy them from me at the shop. I expect you get plenty of butter, cheese and eggs in the country. Give my regards to Mr and Mrs Trewithen.

Well, must sign off now. I hope you liked the birthday card with Trouble on the front.

Love

Auntie Jean

Xxx

I read Auntie's letter one more time, then put it in my knicker drawer. Vera put her head round the bedroom door.

"'Ave you scoffed all the sweets then, Polly?"

"Sorry, no sweets, Vera, just a letter and my lovely card."

"This your cat then – on the card?"

"No, but it looks very much like him."

"Your Auntie OK, is she?"

"Sounds like it, but food's going to be rationed soon and she's not sure what's going to happen to the shop. I think she's a bit worried about that."

"What we goin' to do about the lads, Poll?"

"Well Vera, I think we should tell Mrs M and Denzil. They've been so kind to us all. I'm sure they will know what to do. But before we *do* tell them, I think we should try and find out a bit more about the two women – Mrs Tremaine and the owner. Perhaps we could find an excuse to go up to the Gull House to have a snoop. What do you think?"

"I think that's a grand idea, Poll," and Vera sniffed her approval. "But she *knows* me – Mrs Tremaine – she's bound to remember me," said Vera.

"Vera, you are hardly recognisable in your clean checked dress and your hair in plaits. Nothing like the Vera who was kicked out of Gull House. But don't say anything. Nothing at all, because she will remember your voice, and wear your big sun hat."

Vera and I found our excuse to go up to Gull House the following morning.

"Vera, Polly, would you to do something for me?" Ma asked. "I want to do some preserving for the winter and Mrs Tremaine, the housekeeper at the big house, lets me have her left over pears and peaches from the orchard and I give her a jar or two in return. You will need to be polite though – she's a bit fierce, Mrs Tremaine." Vera winked at me across the table.

***

Climbing the hill from the quay, Vera and I worked out a plan.

"You must do the talkin', Poll – you're the polite one."

"And you, Vera, are the cunning one."

And we climbed the steep hill breathing heavily with exertion and apprehension.

I lifted the large knocker on the front door and the sound reverberated through the house. The open door revealed a tall, thin woman dressed in a long grey skirt and a Fair Isle cardigan just as Vera had described her.

"Yes?" she said curtly, crossing her arms.

"Good morning, Mrs Tremaine. My name is Polly and this is my friend – we are staying at Quay Cottage." To my amusement Vera bobbed a curtsey.

"And?" The thin woman shuffled on two large feet.

"Well, actually all we came for was the leftover fruit you sometimes give to Mrs Trewithen. We will gladly pick the fruit ourselves."

"Take the basket and go round to the back of the house to the orchard and I will let you in through the gate." She turned abruptly to Vera. "Don't I know you, child?"

"Oh, thank you very much," I said quickly. "I'm sure Mrs Trewithen will send up some jars for you." And the woman's attention was diverted from Vera. Vera couldn't stop giggling as we walked to the back of the garden.

"The 'orse-faced old bat. Who does she think she is – Lady Muck!"

"Hush Vera, she'll hear you," I said, as the old oak door in the wall leading to the orchard swung open.

"This way. Mrs Binns the cook is poorly so I will show you how, where, and what to pick." And Mrs Tremaine led the way through the kitchen garden to the orchard.

"You may fill the basket and I don't mind if you eat some whilst you are picking, girls. There's far too much for everyone at the house. And don't make a noise, Mrs Cadle is resting."

"But what about…" I kicked Vera on the ankles. I knew what she was thinking.

"What you do that for, Poll?" said Vera rubbing her ankle after Mrs Tremaine had gone.

"I thought you were going to mention the boys, Vera. Sorry."

"All that food! Did you see the size of the veg patch?"

"Yes – but never mind, let's pick the fruit quickly and maybe we'll get into the house somehow."

"I know," said Vera spluttering over a juicy peach. "We'll ask for the lav – she won't refuse us surely." On our way to the toilet through the back kitchen we had a good view of the large entrance hall. There was no sign of the boys.

"Look at that staircase, Poll – that's grand that is. And look there's a landing and another staircase goin' further up. P'raps that's where the lads sleep."

A bell rang in the kitchen, one of many on the wall. It said bedroom 1 on the label.

"Quick – let's get back to the garden, Vera."

We had seen nothing of Billy and Jack, but we'd had a good view of the entrance and stairs. Mrs Cadle, the owner of the house, must spend most of her time in her bedroom. It was her bell which had rung in the kitchen. The boys hadn't mentioned seeing anything of Mrs Cadle.

Later, Vera and I sat on the bed watching the last rays of sunlight playing on the receding tide. It had been a 'sort of' good day, but we were sad we hadn't seen the boys. Ma was pleased with our pickings.

"Well, time for bed, Vera. I'm *really* tired." I yawned. Vera went to the window and knelt down, elbows on the sill.

"Gull House is in complete darkness now, Polly. I expect Mrs Cadle is already asleep. Is she an invalid? What's the bettin' the lads are still workin'. Wait a mo' – what's that – at the top of the house – 'ere, Poll, come an' 'ave a look."

I joined Vera on my knees and we peeped round the blackout curtain.

"It's a light flashing on and off, Vera. I wonder what that means. Oh it's stopped now." We watched for a while longer until our eyelids began to droop.

Lights, ghosts, stairs – Gull House really was very mysterious. (But at the moment all I could think of was how sore my throat was. I fell asleep with my head bursting.)

CHAPTER 7

"Polly, dear, are you feeling poorly?" Ma was sitting on the bed with a soft hand on my burning forehead.

"I feel awful, Ma, my throat is so sore. I do get lots of sore throats – sorry."

"Don't fret. You must stay in your bed and I'll make up some nice soup and give you some aspirin. I will ask Dr March to come and take a look at you. Vera said she will keep you company while I help Denzil. Fox got two hens last night and we need to mend the fence."

Ma bustled out of my room and left me hot and sweaty, and a bit tearful, but I dozed off eventually.

"Polly – Poll – it's me," said Vera softly. "Here's the aspirin and some cold water."

"Oh, Vera, I feel awful. My throat is… is…" I patted the bed inviting Vera to come closer. "I can't manage the soup, Vera."

"Don't talk if it hurts, Poll. I'll do the talking." Vera lowered herself gently on to the bed, tidying the cover around me. Dear Vera, she was proving to be such a good friend.

"Last night, Poll – after you had gone to sleep I couldn't quite drop off like. You was burning up beside me and – well anyway I got out of bed for a bit and looked out of our window. I saw the light, Poll, again at Gull House, right at the top – just a small window. The rest of the house was in darkness. Anyway I sat and watched for a bit until I got too cold."

"Maybe someone just forgot to turn a bedroom light off," I croaked.

Vera looked thoughtful, fingering the bedcover.

"Well maybe, but it was odd like, when the light kept going on and off. I think it was a lamp or a candle maybe. Anyway, it did stop again after a while. Do you think we should tell anyone?"

"Not just yet, Vera – not yet. Please wait until I'm feeling better," I pleaded.

"Polly, this is Doctor March – he's just come to check up on you dear. Vera, can you go and make Doctor a cup of tea?"

"Open wide," said the doctor, at the same time feeling my neck. "Looks like tonsillitis, young lady. Have you had this before?"

I nodded my yes and buried my head under the cover.

"Lots of cold drinks, young lady – some medicine and a few days in bed should sort you out. Mrs Trewithen will soon get you better. This hot weather doesn't help of course. Try and keep her cool, Mrs Trewithen."

And so I had to languish in bed whilst Vera and the twins helped Ma and Denzil in the house. I wrote to Auntie twice that week and Vera brought me an ice cream from the village shop, when she went to post the letters.

"Bumped into the housekeeper from Gull House, Poll," Vera said excitedly.

"And?" I questioned.

"Well nothing really, but I felt like saying she should watch the blackout and not leave lights on."

"But you didn't – did you, Vera?"

"No – 'course not," Vera sniffed. "But I did ask her how the boys were and if Jack's face was better. She went really red, Poll, and dashed out of the shop."

I thought about what Vera had told me as I lay in bed, the windows wide open on to the quay, a hot breeze brushing past the curtains into the room and the sound, as always, of the seagulls noisily scavenging discarded food. Gull House, perched on the very edge of the cliff, looked bleak, even in the brilliant afternoon sun. Was there a mystery to be revealed or was it just the result of summer boredom? I feel useless lying here but Vera has promised not to do anymore until I am better. We are a team, Vera said, and we have to act together.

CHAPTER 8

I recovered from my tonsillitis just in time to start school! Vera was horrified, but the twins were excited except for having forgotten their times tables.

"But Ma," Vera pleaded, "you need us here, to help you."

"Now Vera, you know full well you have to do your schoolwork and you can do some jobs after you've done your lessons."

"Can we still go to the beach after school?" Rose looked longingly through the kitchen window to the quay.

"Of course, Rose. Tell you what, I'll bring a picnic on Friday after school, and, if the weather's right, we'll eat it either on the quay or on the beach. And *maybe* Denzil will let us eat on the boat sometimes."

Gull House, lighted windows, mysteries went out of our thoughts, for the time being anyway, as the twins caught up on their times tables, coached by me, and I helped Vera with her reading.

"I told you I was a dunce, Poll. I'm stupid." Vera was crestfallen.

"You are definitely not stupid, Vera – just the opposite."

***

It was a glorious autumn day when we climbed the hill to Padstow School. A crocodile of children, assorted ages, carrying our boxed gas masks. The war seemed a very long way away and it felt good to be doing something normal.

"I feel sick, Poll."

"Oh Vera – listen – there are only two big classes so we are bound to be together – do buck up – it's just another adventure." But Vera wasn't convinced.

We sat in the assembly hall with its familiar smell of chalk, wooden flooring, polish, disinfectant and the echoes of excited and anxious voices bouncing off the walls. The windows were too high to catch a glimpse of the sea. The murmuring ceased as the two teachers entered, climbed up front and we all stood.

"I can smell cabbage," Vera whispered. "I hate cabbage."

"Shush, Vera."

"Good morning, everyone."

"Good morning, Miss."

"Welcome to Padstow School. My name is Miss Jones and I am the headmistress and this is Mrs Tregotthan. There are just the two of us, but I'm sure we are all going to manage very well together."

There was an audible sigh of relief in the hall.

"I want you to know that we are aware that there are children with us who are not from this part of the country – that you are far from home – and that we shall do our very best to make you feel comfortable. Cornwall is a beautiful county – Padstow in particular – and you will be safe here. Before we divide into two classes we shall say a prayer, sing a hymn and sing the National Anthem. Good luck, everyone."

One thing was certain – Vera could sing! Standing beside me her voice carried over and above everyone else as she sang the National Anthem with gusto. We smiled at one another and I just knew everything was going to be alright.

Scanning the sea of faces I saw the twins standing very close to one another – they looked fine. However, there was no sign of Billy and Jack from Gull House.

"What's ya names, then?" said the boy standing beside me.

"This is my friend Vera and I'm Polly. What's your name?"

"Brian and I'm ten. You evacuees?"

"Yes. We stay with Mr and Mrs Trewithen in Quay Cottage along with the twins over there."

"Where ya really from then – London?"

"No, Leeds in Yorkshire."

"I told you it was cabbage! I hate cabbage," said Vera, far too loudly.

"We get cabbage nearly every day," volunteered Brian, "but we do get lots of bread pudding. See ya later."

"There you are, Vera – we've already made one new friend."

I turned to Vera, who, to my horror was holding out her plate to the dinner lady, firmly holding her nose.

"Cabbage every day – I'll never see the war out!"

***

Saturday, the postman brought letters for the twins and Vera. "Steady on, girls, there'll be no letter left by the time you've finished with it," said Ma, beaming as the twins tore open theirs.

Vera had found herself a corner by the stove to read hers and for a while there was silence in the kitchen. I brought in the washing and started folding it at the same time scanning Vera's face.

"Well, she seems alright – Mam – and Dad too," said Vera looking up at me.

"There's no news of me brother but Mam says she doesn't expect any yet. She says everybody's moaning about the petrol rationing, but wc don't 'ave a car so Dad's not bothered. *But* it means everything's more expensive – food especially." And then Vera laughed, her thin shoulders shaking.

"Mam said there was a practice air raid with sirens and everything, and when they closed the door on the shelter mi Dad was missing! Mam says he got caught short and was in the lavvy next door! Mi poor Dad – ya have to laugh."

And we did.

"What about your letter, girls – everything alright at home?" I asked Rose and Nellie.

"Please Polly, will you read it – we can't understand our Mam's writing?"

"My dear girls,

It was lovely to get your letter. Please thank Denzil for helping you write it.

Everything is fine at the moment except I do miss you very much. Your Dad isn't far away – only Harrogate – but he may be going to Scotland to train. He does look handsome in his uniform though. He sends you love and kisses and is pleased you are together and in such a lovely place. Don't forget to save us some seashells.

Before Dad left he put the car away in the garage. I can't drive and petrol's now rationed so it doesn't matter really. But he did find Mary – your doll, Rose – sitting on the back seat. I put her on your bed dear for when you come home.

"I should have brought her, I should have brought her." Rose, close to tears, clutched Nellie's hand.

"She is safe with Mam, Rose, don't cry," said her sister.

"The letter's nearly finished, Rose, shall I read it?"

Rose nodded a 'yes'.

Now girls, remember your manners and don't forget to wear your vests even if it feels warm. I will write again soon or maybe send you a postcard.

Your ever loving Mother

xxxx

CHAPTER 9

"I want to go and find some seashells for Mam. Polly, will you take us to the beach?" Rose pleaded.

"Can we take them, Ma?" I asked.

"You can – fresh air will do you all good especially you Polly, after being cooped up in bed. Get some roses in those pale cheeks!"

Ma gave us the basket for the shells and waved us off.

"Mind the tide, girls!" she shouted after us. "Back in one hour please."

Vera had hitched her skirt up into her knickers before we left the quay, she was so excited. The twins held hands, as always, heads close together chattering.

I looked across the quay to Rock. We hadn't explored Rock yet but Denzil had promised to take us across in his boat before the autumn tides. I felt the sand firm and cool under my feet and I watched the twins lifting rocks and, with squeals of delight, releasing scurrying crabs from their shelter.

Surely we would all remember this time here in lovely Cornwall with its wide, brilliant blue sky, the threat of war so distant, I no longer felt that heavy bruising loss for home but wished Auntie and Trouble could be here to share it with me. I must write another letter tonight. I sat on a rock with my toes in the cold sea water and shivered a little – it was getting late. I couldn't see the twins, only Vera searching for crabs. "Vera, where are the girls? It's almost time we left – look at the tide it's coming closer!" I shouted.

Vera waved, ran forward a little then disappeared out of sight. Where had they gone! Vera reappeared waving her arms frantically beckoning me to hurry. They had found a cave!

"Polly quick – it's huge, huge, huge, huge, huge, huge, huge!" her voice echoed.

The sand under my toes was unexpectedly dry. I looked back though the cave entrance. I thought the tide looked much closer – I could see the white tips of the rollers.

"Where are the twins – Vera, we must get out quickly or we will be cut off by the tide?"

"TWINS!" – Vera roared and the echo repeated twins, twins, twins, twins.

"Come and look, Vera, we found something." Rosie's voice reverberated through the cave.

"Whatever it is, Vera? We must be quick."

Vera sensed the urgency finally, and went further into the cave to get the girls.

I waited anxiously watching the approaching waves.

"Come on girls." Vera dragged Rose and Nellie. "Best hurry up, or 'ee'll get caught."

I turned and saw a figure standing at the entrance with the light behind him.

"We need to get round the point." It was Brian from school.

"Come ON, girls!" Vera dragged Rose and Nellie along the beach behind Brian.

"What was in there, Vera?" I whispered.

"Tell you when we get back, Poll. HURRY girls!"

We leapt and slipped over the rocks and away from the approaching waves.

"Follow me!" yelled Brian. "We need to get up Ruthian Steps." And Brian lifted Nellie piggy back and we followed close behind, dragging Rose along between us.

CHAPTER 10

Leaving Brian on the cliff top, Vera was able to tell me what the twins had found.

"Steps winding steps through the back of the cave and disappearing around a corner. We should go back and see where they lead to – not today though."

I don't think Ma even noticed we were a bit late and dishevelled. She and Denzil sat at the kitchen table, heads close together.

"Get a wash, girls, and come and have a bite to eat."

Denzil and Ma stopped talking as soon as we came into the kitchen. Denzil looked a bit fierce and Ma was quite pale.

"Anything wrong, Denzil?" I said pulling a chair up beside him.

"Oh, nothing to worry a bonny maid like 'ee Polly. Eat that good bread and cheese now." And brushing his hand gently over the twins' hair as he passed, Denzil waved goodbye.

"Now you rascals, you didn't think I'd missed you comin' back did 'ee?"

"Sorry Ma, we were so busy collecting shells for Rose and Nellie, we almost missed the tide coming, but Brian, from school, he took care of us – didn't he twins?"

"We found a cave, Ma," Nellie piped up. And I groaned under my breath.

"Did 'ee indeed. And would that be the one under the cliffs about a mile below Gull House near Ruthian Steps?"

"Ye, yes that's the one, Ma," said Vera. "But we didn't realise it was anywhere near Gull House."

"Well you can't see it, you see, from the beach because of the overhanging cliffs. It's called the Siren's Cave."

"What's a Siren?" asked a wide eyed Nellie.

"A Siren, me 'andsome, is like a water fairy but she has a tail like a mermaid and they have a beautiful singing voice."

"Oooh, ooh!" said the twins in unison.

"There are many tales about Sirens in these parts luring young sailors away to their deaths in the sea. Very beautiful they are, girls – just like you!" Ma put an arm around the twins and squeezed.

"I want to be a Siren," Rose piped up.

"Me too – me too," followed Nellie.

"You 'aven't got tails, dafties." And Vera laughed.

"The story goes…" began Ma and Nellie planted herself on Ma's knee leaving no room for Rose who promptly sat on Vera.

"Your knickers are wet, Rose!" said Vera.

"Sh-sh Vera, listen to Ma," said a wriggling Rose.

"The story goes that long ago a Siren lured to his death the one and only son of the people living at Gull House. He disappeared one day when fishing off the rocks near the cave and – the story goes – there was beautiful singing heard right over to Rock. He was never seen again, but on the anniversary of his disappearance many people have heard the beautiful voice of the Siren. Now off you go and finish your chores. Them 'ens are fair starving with neglect!"

Feeding the hens, Vera and I talked about the Siren.

"Do you suppose the ghost at Gull House is the ill-fated son?" said Vera dramatically.

"I shouldn't think so – sounds like a baby elephant! I think Ma told us that story to warn us off visiting the cave anymore. What I want to know is – what were Ma and Denzil whispering about in the kitchen?"

CHAPTER 11

"I'm really 'ungry, Billy," Jack rubbed his scrawny belly.

"Me too – she'll be 'ere soon though, our Jack."

"What's she doin' keeping us up 'ere, Billy? I don't like 'er – the housekeeper."

"It's 'cos we saw that fella – ya know – goin' up them back stairs. Looked a bit of a villain to me 'e did. But I don't know why she should think we're bothered. Nowt to do with us."

The sound of the door being unlocked turned Jack's attention away from his hunger.

"Now lads, I've brought you your supper. Good sized pasties – one each and a big jug of milk." It was Mrs Binns the cook.

"Why 'ave we got to stay 'ere, Mrs Binns – we've done nowt wrong?" said Billy.

"I can't say, lads. Ask no questions and you won't hear lies."

"Well 'ow long, Mrs Binns? Our Jack's gettin' upset and when 'e gets upset 'e chucks up."

"Chucks up – what do you mean chucks up?"

"You know he's sick everywhere." Billy did a good impression of Jack being sick.

"Now don't fret, boys – it won't be for long. Everything will be sorted out in a day or two you'll see. Now eat up and have a look at those comic books I brought you – there's good bairns." And Mrs Binns locked the door behind her.

"She forgot to take the chamber pot with 'er," said Jack biting a good size chunk out of his pastie.

CHAPTER 12

"Fancy seeing you, Brian," said Vera. We were at the Post Office sending off more letters home.

"I've been off school with a bad cold – alright now though," said Brian.

"Have you heard about the big robbery in Plymouth?"

"What robbery – where's Plymouth?" said Vera sniffing very loudly.

"You know, Vera, where we crossed over the Brunel Bridge on our way to Padstow." And of course Vera remembered.

"Big one – at the Armaments Depot. I heard it on the radio the other day," said Brian.

"I'll bet that was what Denzil and Ma were whispering about, Vera."

"Dead serious it is," said Brian lowering his voice. "Nearly wiped out the whole depot and nobody knows yet where they've got to."

"You talkin' about guns and things Brian?" Vera lowered her voice.

"Worse than that. Things that can wipe out the whole of Cornwall in a blink," said Brian importantly.

"Don't frighten Vera Brian, or she'll have dreams," I said, worried that Vera's snoring might turn to screams.

"Well I'm only tellin' you what I know. Anyway, got to be off – see ya at school."

Vera and I posted our letters and walked back to the cottage. Cornwall was such a peaceful place. I couldn't imagine anything or anyone disturbing that peace. Why would anyone want to hurt Denzil and Ma and all the lovely people we had met? And we had been sent here from the big cities because it was safe. Brian was probably fibbing. I will ask Denzil what he thinks. "Don't dawdle, Vera, we'll be late for supper – race you!"

Vera beat me, of course, skirt hitched up inside her knickers. We both fell inside the kitchen laughing our heads off.

"Steady on, girls." Ma lurched forward as we flew through the door. "Sorry, Ma we were racing. What's for supper please?"

"Chicken stew with dumplings, Cornish style," and we saw her smile as she turned away.

"Ma."

"Yes, Polly?"

"We saw Brian at the Post Office and he said there had been a big robbery in Plymouth, at the Armaments Depot." Ma hesitated as she served the vegetable stew and dumplings and took a seat at the table.

"I thought you said it was chicken, Ma?" Vera asked plaintively.

"Hush, Vera, let Ma speak."

"Couldn't bring myself to wring our Judy's neck – not yet anyway. You can 'ave some cheese and bread at bedtime if you're still hungry, Vera."

"Now Polly – where did young Brian get that news?"

"On the radio Ma or so he said."

"Well he's right. There was a big robbery last week. I expect the police 'ave caught them villains though, you see."

"Brian said they took bombs big enough to flatten Cornwall," a wide-eyed Vera said.

"Lot of nonsense girls. Now eat up and maybe I'll make some custard. That stew looks a bit thin."

.

CHAPTER 13

"Can't sleep, Polly – me tums rumbling and gurgling. Must 'ave been the stew. What you doin' out of bed?"

"Come here, Vera – come and look."

I sat next to Vera under the window and she saw straight away what I meant.

"It's that flashing light and it's coming from upstairs in Gull House again. But, Vera – that's not all – look, further to the left over the quay out to sea – can you see anything?"

"No I can't – oh! Wait – yes!"

"Another light, Vera, but not flashing as often. In fact, it's stopped altogether now. But there is a bit of a hump showing."

"What do you mean *hump* Polly?"

"Like a small island or something."

Vera had forgotten all about her rumbling tummy and was sniffing excitedly beside me.

"Vera, you stay here – I'm going to get Denzil. There's something not quite right about this."

"But maybe Denzil and Ma have noticed the light from the house."

"I don't think so, Vera. Their bedroom looks out the back over the garden. Anyway I'm going downstairs first to see if they're still up and then I'm going to knock on their bedroom door!" And I left Vera keeping a lookout and slipped quietly downstairs so as not to wake the twins.

The kitchen was empty.

"Polly, what are you doing up at this time?" Ma came through the kitchen door wrapped up in her shawl.

"I want to show Denzil something, Ma – or you."

"Denzil isn't here, Polly – he had to go out to look at the moorings. He thinks there might be a storm brewing. Now off to bed this instant."

"But…" I stuttered.

"No buts, you can tell Denzil whatever it is in the morning."

"But it…"

"This instant, Polly."

It was no use arguing with Ma. Denzil had to be the one and it might as well wait until morning now.

"Goodnight, Ma."

"Night night, Polly – there's a good girl."

Vera was none too pleased with me.

"But I thought you said it was important, Poll."

"It's Denzil we need to tell, Vera, so it will have to wait until morning. Go back to sleep."

"But Polly."

"What?"

"Oh never mind," said Vera, crawling back into our bed and curling her freezing legs around mine.

CHAPTER 14

The storm continued to rage for another two nights, and Denzil only came home briefly for more clothes. The twins didn't go to school because of nasty colds and huddled together around the fire grate, Ma fussing and cooing, filling them with hot drinks.

"Vera, I think we should go to the house."

"What in this 'orrible weather?" Vera sulked.

"We have to see the boys. I know Ma and Denzil are worried but Ma won't leave the twins. We'll tell her where we're going, Vera."

As I expected Ma wasn't pleased, but she gave us jars of bottled pears to take with us.

"Don't be long now girls or I'll be worried. It's getting dark." Wrapped warmly in oilskins and boots, Vera and I braved the high winds and climbed the hill to Gull House. The sound of the door knocker reverberated through the house and there was a long pause before the big door opened on to a white faced Mrs Binns.

"Whatever are you two doin' out on a night like this?"

"Can we come in, Mrs Binns – just for a moment?" I held up the jars of pears.

"Well just for a minute – I've got things to do."

"Where are the boys, Mrs Binns, Jack and Billy? We haven't seen them at school for ages?"

"They – er – they got chicken pox – very contagious chicken pox is – not right to send them off to school."

"Can we see them, Mrs Binns? I've had chicken pox and you have, Vera, I remember you told me so – very spotty, you said."

"I never…"

I kicked Vera's ankle.

"I never 'ad anythin' so bad in all me life," said Vera beaming.

"Well anyway – I'm sorry girls, but they're too poorly." And Mrs Binns very firmly led us to the door.

Standing outside the house, the rain lashing down on our heads and the wind blowing us almost off our feet, Vera and I decided to try and get into the house through the back kitchen door. We couldn't leave; we just knew the boys were in danger.

"What a pack of lies, Poll," Vera whispered, as we crept to the rear of the building.

"I know Vera. But what on earth is going on?" I lifted the latch of the back door. Thankfully it was open. We dripped rain as we climbed the back stairs to what must be the attic. There was a small door at the head of the stairs. It was then we heard raised voices. Vera put her fingers to her lips and put her ear to the door.

"It's the lads – one of 'ems crying," Vera whispered.

"GOTYA!!"

The housekeeper laid a hand on my shoulder and at the same time grabbed Vera's wrist. She then threw open the door and pushed us in. Billy and Jack were trussed up like turkeys, attached to the wall pipes.

"Who are they?" said a man jumping to his feet from a trundle bed at the back of the room.

"Prying little eyes. We haven't got time to sort this out now – tie them up with the kids. You do what you have to do and I'll sort this lot out with the cook and the owner." The man opened a second door in the room and disappeared.

"Keep quiet and you will come to no harm." The housekeeper spat the words out at the same time binding our wrists to the pipes. She left, locking the door behind her.

"I want me Mam, our Billy!" Poor Jack, his grubby face streaked with tears looked at his brother.

"'E's bin sayin' that for two days," Billy said, his voice trembling.

Vera tried to shuffle a little closer to Jack to comfort him, but the ropes binding her wrists were too tight.

"Try to behave, boys. Ma will tell Denzil where we are and he'll come soon. Won't he, Polly?"

I only hoped the boys hadn't picked up the fear in Vera's voice.

CHAPTER 15

"I don't know what the time is, Vera, but Ma must surely be missing us by now. We've been gone ages."

I tried to rub my wrist. The bonds were too tight making my hands go numb. I stopped with the sound of the door being opened. In came the housekeeper with Mrs Binns and they were arguing.

"But you can't keep the bairns trussed up like that. Those boys need some food and water. Let me get them something to eat. I'll bring it straight back up here and you can lock me in with them if you like," said Mrs Binns.

"Very well, Mrs Binns, you can go and do what you want. I want you back up here in five minutes or I will pay Mrs Cadle a visit."

The housekeeper then unlocked the door once more and Mrs Binns hurried down the stairs.

"Can I 'ave some cheese and pickle – I like cheese and pickle don't I, our Billy?" said Jack plaintively.

"You'll 'ave what you're given and like it, or you'll get another slap!" spat the housekeeper.

"Shurrup Jack," was all Billy had to say.

Mrs Binns was back in no time.

"Here you are, boys, some nice bread and cheese and a cup of milk."

"You'll have to untie them 'cos I'm not feedin' them," said Mrs Binns to the housekeeper.

"Alright – but be quick."

"Girls, I've got you the same."

"Thank you, Mrs Binns, you are very kind," I said pointedly.

The second door was flung open.

"I need your help – you'll have to leave them and come with me. What's she doing here?" asked the man pointing to Mrs Binns.

"The kids needed food," the housekeeper answered him.

"Hurry up. The tides right and the winds are abating," said the man.

"I'm coming, I'm coming. If you don't do as you're told, cook, we'll take Mrs Cadle with us for a little boat ride."

"Oh – can we come for a boat ride?"

"Shurrup, our Jack!!"

"Don't worry – I won't leave the bairns," said Mrs Binns, rubbing Jack's red wrist between her hands, and the door closed leaving Mrs Binns with the four of us.

"Mrs Binns, you're not doing anything wrong are you?" I asked.

"Bless you, no dear. But it's been hard these past months – trying to keep my mouth shut. 'E's a nasty piece of work, Mrs Tremaine's nephew. 'E said 'e would hurt Mrs Cadle, the dear soul, and I think he meant it. Whatever 'e's up to – it's important."

"That awful man is the housekeeper's nephew? Flippin' 'eck!" said Vera. "Mind you she's a bad un 'erself," and Vera sniffed louder than ever.

"They are both German sympathisers," said Mrs Binns. "'E's very clever – an engineer I think. I'm sure they had somethin' to do with the robbery in Plymouth. You know – at the Armaments Depot? There's been some rum goings on these past weeks since 'e's been livin' in the attic."

"So there never was a ghost walkin' about over the boys' room?" said Vera.

"Bless you, no – nothin' ghostly about *that* man."

"Now – eat up quick, because we're gettin' out of here," said Mrs Binns, grinning. "The old battle-axe doesn't know I've got a spare key to every door in this 'ouse." She untied the boys as she spoke.

"Girls, help me push this bed behind the small door. It's the only door I can't lock."

We all helped Mrs Binns push the trundle bed across the room with the table on top.

"Why are we doin' this, Mrs Binns?" I asked.

"So they can't get back up here. There's a little surprise waiting for them on the beach."

"Oooh – our Billy – it's just like a comic adventure," Jack said.

"Shurrup Jack."

"OK everyone, follow me. You need to go to the back of the house," said Mrs Binns, wiping her face with her apron.

"Why?" we all said in unison.

"You'll see – now come on, quick!"

"What about Mrs Cadle?" I asked.

"She's alright, Polly – we'll come back for her, dear."

***

We followed Mrs Binns down the narrow stairs until we reached the second landing. Then down the main stairs – the grand staircase the housekeeper had called it, and finally through the hall and into the kitchen. Mrs Binns unlocked the back door and we almost fell out into the kitchen garden.

"Not done yet, girls – come on – hurry!" shouted Mrs Binns above the wind.

"I can't see, it's too dark," said Billy.

Through the garden we bumped straight into the arms of a huge figure.

"Denzil, oh Denzil, it's you."

Vera and I threw our arms around Denzil's waist.

"This is Billy and this is Jack," said Vera, pushing the boys in front of Denzil.

"They were prisoners in Gull House." I could hear the sobs in Vera's voice.

"Alright, alright me 'andsomes. Now go with my friend 'ere. There's a police car waiting for you." It was Brian's dad standing with Denzil. "Mrs Binns and I will go and fetch Mrs Cadle from the house. I'll have to carry her. You can come back later – I just want you all out of harm's way."

"But what about the housekeeper and her nephew – they went down the tunnel to the beach?" I said.

"There are policemen, coastguards and Home Guard down on the beach waiting for them, Polly. I'll join them when I've seen you're safe. I don't want you anywhere near the beach, the tide's high so they can transfer their er…er… – goods to another dinghy."

"But where are they going?" Vera pleaded in the dark.

"You're asking too many questions Vera. Now scoot – all of ya," and Denzil gave us a firm nudge.

"I'm not missin' all the fun, Poll – are you comin' with me?" said Vera into my ear.

"We've been *told* what to do, Vera," I whispered.

"Er… er… Mrs Binns – I've left me waterproof in the kitchen and it's the only one I've got – I'm just going to fetch it." And before Mrs Binns could even reply, Vera grabbed my hand and dragged me back through the darkness.

We followed the path which led down to the beach, all the time fighting the wind.

"We'll get into real trouble, Vera," I said over the roaring wind.

"Come on Polly – we can't miss out. I want to know what all this is about."

The path leading to the beach was narrow – too narrow to hold hands. Anyway I could barely feel my fingers. There were too many clouds covering the moon to give us light as we slipped and scurried down the path and Vera was going too fast for me to keep up. I could hear her breathing though and trying to stifle her loud sniffs. She must be freezing without a coat.

Then we turned a corner through the gorse and saw the beach below just as the thick clouds rolled away from the moon. There were men – just as Denzil had said, but they were hidden behind the rocks. We could see them clearly from where we were above the beach *and* the mouth of the cave from which a figure appeared, hauling a dinghy on to the small amount of beach left by the tide. He pulled it along on wheels and when he reached the water he shed the wheels before jumping in.

"Vera, look – out to sea – it's that hump again, the one we saw from Quay Cottage."

A shaft of moonlight made the grey mound clearly visible.

"Vera, Vera I can't see you – where are you?"

My heart thumped in my chest as I scrambled through the gorse trying to find Vera. Where on earth had she disappeared to? The gorse scratched my legs as I carefully retraced my steps to find the place where I had last heard her voice. Then the moon, once more, vanished behind thick clouds leaving me in total darkness.

I pushed back the hood of my coat listening for Vera, but all I could hear was the sea, wind and rustling shrubbery. Raised voices rose up from the beach but I concentrated hard, listening for my friend's voice.

At last I heard a cry, hollow like an echo – it was Vera alright – no mistaking Vera's voice!

"Polly – Polleee!" she yelled. "Where the heck are ya? Get me out of this hole." I moved towards Vera's cries and almost fell into the hole myself!

"Vera, are you alright?" I called, creeping as close as I dare to the edge.

"'Course I'm not alright. I'm stuck aren't I and I can 'ear water below me."

"I'll go and get help, Vera – we need a rope or something to pull you out."

"Don't you dare leave me, Poll, or I'll never be your friend ever *EVER* again."

"But we need help, Vera – I promise I will be back as quickly as I possibly can."

"Alright then, but 'urry up, Poll, I don't like it down 'ere and I'm really cold."

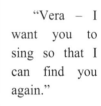

"Vera – I want you to sing so that I can find you again."

"SING – don't be daft – I don't feel like singing – just get me OUT!!"

"Vera, trust me. If you sing I will be able to find the hole again. I know – pretend you are Alice in Wonderland and you have just slipped down a rabbit hole."

"If there are any flippin' rabbits an' things down 'ere – I really will scream."

And so I crawled away from the hole to the sound of Vera bravely singing the National Anthem with considerable gusto.

CHAPTER 16

I blundered through the gorse trying to find the path which led down to the beach. At one point as the clouds scurried past the moon I found I was dangerously close to the edge of the cliff. The sound of Vera's singing became fainter and I wondered if it was going to be possible to find the hole again. Panic rose up to my throat and my eyes stung with tears.

"Please, please help me!" I pleaded into the wind. The idea hit me immediately. I whipped off my scarf and tied it clumsily around a bush in the dark. Then further on I took off my coat and laid it across the gorse. The wind bit into my chest as I struggled with first one sock and then another. Someone fired a flare on the beach and this helped me descend the last few feet.

"Dear Heaven, Polly, where on earth have you been?" And at once Denzil's arms were around me as I sank gratefully into his chest.

"We are so sorry, Denzil," I whispered. "Vera and I wanted to see what was happening and so we didn't go to the back of the house as you said."

"And where is Vera, Polly?" Denzil whispered into my hair.

"She fell down a hole further up the hill where the path is – I don't think it's very far – it was so hard for me to see where I was going, but she's really frightened, Denzil, and very cold. We need a rope or something to get her out."

"Sounds as if she has found St Agnes mine."

"What's that, Denzil?"

"Disused tin mine, Polly – there are still passages which haven't been filled in. Hasn't been used in years, trust Vera to fall into one."

"What are we going to do, Denzil?"

"Get help and then you and I will track back up to the mine. Are you sure you can find the way back?"

I told Denzil about leaving the trail of clothes.

"Well done – 'ere 'ave my jacket. My socks will be too big for 'ee. Now stay 'ere – do as you're told, Polly." Swallowed up in Denzil's coat, I sank gratefully to my knees. Denzil was going to take care of everything.

CHAPTER 17

What followed next was a rush of activity on the beach. Huddled in Denzil's coat, I peered through the gloom below me. Someone fired a gun followed by another and searchlights swung over the water until the dinghy was lit up as if by daylight. The man stood up in the inflatable, firing a handgun back into the crowd of men. The dinghy rocked from side to side and I could see from above that it was filled with boxes.

"Halt – you are covered – go no further. Put down your arms!" A megaphone roared across the sea but the dinghy now moved faster, an outboard motor, at first chugging and hesitating, came to life. He was going to get away – to the grey hump still waiting for him on the horizon.

I don't know who fired the next shot but it was aimed right at the dinghy and its cargo. The explosion filled the darkness, lighting up the cave below. There were further explosions and there was nothing to see at the end but smoke and flotsam covering the surface of the sea. A great silence filled the air. The man and his dinghy had gone, along with his precious, deadly cargo. The searchlights scanned the water beyond but the grey hump disappeared quietly below the waves and would soon be miles away. The man had been useful to the enemy, to a point, but unsuccessful in the end game. Did they care, I wondered? Someone else would replace him soon enough. I was reminded that we were at war. Thinking the drama had reached its climax I was surprised when, once again, voices were raised below. And then I saw a figure appear at the mouth of the cave. She sank to her knees in the sand and, even though I was far away from the beach, I could hear her cries of distress cut into the darkness. It was surely the housekeeper. Her nephew was dead and she was surrounded by armed men. I felt a sudden rush of sadness. Why, I did not know.

"Polly, come with me my 'andsome. Never mind what's going on below. It's 'Operation Rescue Vera' now!"

CHAPTER 18

Above the voices of those on the beach Denzil's boomed out over the cliff edge.

"Hey – down there – help needed – child trapped in the mine. I need men and a rope, NOW!!"

Denzil and I were joined by Brian's father and two others.

"Let me come, Denzil – please!" I pleaded.

"Of course, Polly, but be very careful where you step."

And my hand was held firmly in Denzil's large one as we moved forward in the dark together. The torch soon picked out my first sock.

"This way lads."

And then the second sock clinging to the gorse.

"That was a crackin' idea of yours. Well done Polly."

And just as dawn was breaking, with the first hint of daylight behind us, we stumbled on to my jacket blown to the ground by the wind.

"We can't be very far away now, Denzil."

Denzil scanned the ground with his torch looking for my scarf, holding firmly on to my hand.

"Denzil, I can't hear Vera. I told her to sing so that we could find her."

"She's probably too exhausted to sing now, Polly. Come on, we must find her quickly. Folla me, men – not far now. Here's your, scarf Poll."

Finally, in the ever increasing light from behind the hills, we crowded around the hole on our knees.

"Vera, Vera, it's Denzil 'ere. We'll soon get you out, me dear. Give us a shout Vera."

"I've wet me knickers I'm so flippin' freezing." Vera's voice was faint but she was OK.

"Oh, Vera – it's Polly. Just be brave a little bit longer. Denzil will get you out." I called down the hole – the tears coursing down my cheeks.

"She's about twenty feet down, lads. Make a slip knot in that rope and we'll try and get 'er to put it round 'er waist."

"Now, Vera, do as I say and we'll soon 'ave ya out. Put the rope around your waist and we'll pull you up. Alright me 'andsome?"

"Me 'ands are freezing Denzil, an' I can't feel me legs!" Vera's voice was weak and shaky.

"Do your best, Vera – 'ere comes the rope."

And the thick rope disappeared into the dark hole.

"There isn't enough room for us to be lowered down to help, Polly. Vera must do this herself." Brian's father knelt beside me and put his arms around my shoulders.

"Vera," I called down to my friend. "Vera, do your best. I know you can do it."

But no sound came up from the hole.

"The rope must have reached her by now," said one of the men.

"I've done it, Denzil. The rope is round me middle!" There was a sharp tug on the rope and a restrained cheer from the men. Slowly and carefully the men pulled Vera out and she appeared in the torchlight, dirty, her face tear-stained but grinning from ear to ear.

"'Ave I missed anythin'?" she asked, through chattering teeth.

"Just a bit, love," said Brian's dad, wrapping Vera in a big blanket and lifting her in his arms like a babe.

CHAPTER 19

Over a hot cup of cocoa and sitting close to a roaring grate with Ma cooing and clucking around her, Vera recovered from her ordeal. The twins sat at her feet each clutching a leg as if to make sure she didn't leave the house again. She and I had been transported back to the cottage by ambulance having first been to Newquay Cottage Hospital where Vera was declared remarkably well considering her adventure. However, Vera was none too pleased to have missed 'the goings on' as Ma called it.

"It's not fair," Vera declared sniffing loudly.

"There you are, Vera. Now you've caught a cold. I'll need to get something for your chest," said Ma bustling out of the kitchen.

"I *haven't* got a cold." Vera sneezed into one of Denzil's giant handkerchiefs.

We were all despatched to bed, each with hot water bottles. The twins wanted to come into our bedroom but Ma packed them off to their own beds. Vera and I were treated to two lovely wet kisses from Rose and Nellie. Vera climbed in beside me warming her feet on mine and clutching her bottle to her scrawny chest.

"What's that horrible smell, Vera?"

"It's goose fat. Ma insisted on slapping some on me chest to keep away the dreaded chest cold. Never mind that, Poll – TELL!!"

And so I told the story of the night's 'happenings' ending with the explosion in the sea and the disappearing dinghy.

"Honestly, Vera – I was more concerned about you. You could have died down that hole. I thought Denzil and the other men were brilliant, don't you, Vera?"

"'Course I do." Vera sniffed but this time blew her nose.

"Will she go to prison, Poll – the housekeeper?"

"Oh I expect so. She's a spy really, Vera."

"Well I never. Who would have thought we could get caught up in all that? Do you think we'll be in the – *Newquay Herald?*"

"I'm not sure we're supposed to say anything about it. Not till Denzil says so anyway. It will all come out though I'm sure. Vera, were you really frightened in that hole? I would have been sick. I hate small spaces."

Vera, cuddled closer and, trying to ignore the revolting smell of warm goose fat, I listened for a while until she became sleepy.

"It was 'orrible. It really was. I thought about me Mam and Dad and even me brother. I 'eard somewhere that ya whole life flashes past when you're dying."

"Vera, don't be so dramatic. I wouldn't have let you die down a hole."

And Vera giggled into my shoulder.

"Tell you what though. I 'eard something strange, Poll."

"WHAT?"

"Oh I think I'm too tired to tell ya."

"Don't you dare fall asleep – not yet, Vera. What did you hear?"

"Well, Poll. It was when I was singing. I stopped for a bit to get me breath like and I heard it clear as anything."

"Vera, for heaven's sake, WHAT did you hear?"

"It was 'er."

"Who?"

"The Siren. I 'eard the Siren. It was beautiful – a beautiful sweet voice but I couldn't understand what she was saying." And Vera yawned loudly.

"Oh my goodness. You're not fibbin', Vera, are you?"

"'Course not – tell you later, Poll, I'm dead tired."

And Vera fell asleep against my shoulder smelling to high heaven. But she was safe and we could chat in the morning. But it was nearly dinnertime.

Waves of exhaustion swept over me and, drifting into sleep, I heard the gulls outside our window – or was it the Siren – and the sound of blasts above the wind and the woman's cries on the beach.

CHAPTER 20

"Wake up, girls, you have visitors," said Ma peeping around the bedroom door.

"What's the time, Ma?" I asked through half closed eyes.

"It's six o'clock, Polly – tea time. You and Vera have slept for sixteen hours, bless you."

Opening the curtains on to the blue sky and ever present seagulls swooping past the window, an unexpected surge of warmth filled my body.

"Vera, Vera wake up, we have visitors. Come on, put your pullover on and – here let me brush your hair."

"Give over, Poll, I'm half asleep." Vera disappeared under the sheet and then reappeared.

"Did you say – visitors – is it me Mam?"

"I don't think so, but come on downstairs and we'll soon find out."

The kitchen smelt of hot soup and warm scones and the kettle bounced and sang on the hob.

"Mrs Binns!" Vera wrapped her arms around Mrs Binns' waist pushing her face into her ample bosom.

"Dear me child, whatever is that smell?" Mrs Binns said over Vera's head.

"I put goose fat on Vera's chest, Mrs Binns. She was half dead when she came out of that mine shaft. My mother swore by goose fat to keep off the bad chest. Cup of tea, Mrs Binns?"

"Thank you – that would be grand. There are more visitors for you, girls, if you feel up to it," said Mrs Binns, sipping out of one of Ma's best china tea cups and helping herself to a scone. At once two faces appeared at the kitchen door and Billy and Jack slipped shyly into the room.

"Oh boys – oh Billy and Jack, you look – well, you look lovely," I said.

The boys had been scrubbed clean, were wearing smart clothes, but they were both terribly thin.

"Come on, boys, tuck in," said Ma filling the plate with more scones.

"The dears, look at 'em – so hungry and thin. What a wicked woman that housekeeper is, Mrs Binns. Where is she now?"

"Gone to Plymouth and that's all I know. I was questioned a bit by the police, but they let me and the boys go with Mrs Cadle to a lovely hotel in Newquay, just for the present until it's decided we can go back to Gull House. I'll look after the boys of course."

"I was scared stiff, Polly," Jack whispered beside me already on his third scone.

"So was I, Poll. All those policemen and army people with guns on the beach. Someone took us away with Mrs Binns to Newquay Police Station and then to the Cottage Hospital, but best of all they took us up to this lovely hotel and we had a big bath and loads of hot water and this waiter man came to the room with a trolley filled with food – bread, milk, jam, cakes and 'e called me 'young man' like I was somebody special," Billy rattled on, his eyes bright with excitement, and then he paused. "We thought you and Vera was dead, Polly. We seemed to have lost you in the scuffle and dark," he added.

"It's all over, Billy. It's finished. Everything will settle down soon," and I wrapped my arms around both boys and Vera joined in.

"What's that 'orrible smell, Vera?" asked Jack holding his nose.

"It's goose fat on my chest to keep me warm, Jack."

"I'd rather 'ave a lovely hot bath in *our* hotel," said Jack importantly. And the kitchen was filled with relieved laughter.

CHAPTER 21

After our visitors left with a promise to come again soon, Denzil arrived home. He looked tired, but not too tired to have each of the twins bounce on his lap full of questions. Ma had packed them off to a neighbour earlier so that Vera and I could get some rest. Now they were feeling left out.

News travelled fast in the close knit community and before long we had a newspaper reporter visit Quay Cottage and almost the whole of the story was published in the *Newquay Herald*.

"The grey hump was a U-boat, girls – a submarine and the dinghy was carrying armaments – of a secret variety stolen from the Depot in Plymouth," said Denzil. "The man killed wasn't the housekeeper's nephew, he was her son and they were both German spies. The whole thing was carefully planned for a long time. But no-one, least of all the housekeeper, expected our brave *and* nosy girls to get involved. The poor boys were just in the wrong place at the wrong time. The housekeeper had to take some evacuees in as the officials would have become suspicious. Anyway, the police and the army are happy that the news should be released. It was, after all, a victory all round."

"I think you should write to your families, girls, and send a copy of the *Herald* with your photographs. We are so proud of you and I expect they will be too," said Ma, dabbing the corner of her eye with her apron.

The first day back at school was filled with questions. The headmistress even gave permission for a little party with balloons and some jam sandwiches. A great banner in the main hall said: **'WELL DONE, POLLY, VERA, BILLY AND JACK. WE ARE PROUD YOU ARE PUPILS AT PADSTOW SCHOOL'.** The twins, of course, were very cross they didn't get a mention! But they did come to the party.

***

At the weekend Vera and I made our first visit to the beach since the 'goings on'. Taking off our shoes we paddled in the shallows, Vera's skirt, as usual, tucked in her knickers. We held hands as we waded through the gently lapping water.

"Everything's back to normal, Vera. There's no sign of flotsam in the water, the grey hump is long gone and even Gull House looks normal, with the sun shining on it." Vera glanced up at Gull House and sniffed gently.

"When I 'eard the Siren, Poll, I thought that I was the one that was goin' to die, but it was that spy."

"Vera, you know Denzil said it was the noise of running water through the mine shaft that made that singing sound – not a Siren."

"Well *I* 'eard 'er and it *wasn't* water," said Vera loftily. "Last one back to Quay Cottage washes up the dishes," said Vera, hitching her skirt even higher and tearing up the beach ahead of me.

EPILOGUE

By January 1940 almost sixty per cent of evacuees returned to their homes.

A second evacuation effort was started after the Germans had taken over most of France. From June 13th to June 18th 1940 around 100,000 children were evacuated (in many cases re-evacuated).

By the end of 1941, city centres, especially London, became safer.

From June 1944 the Germans attacked again by firing VI rockets on Britain, followed later by V2 rockets. One million women, children, elderly and disabled people were evacuated from London. This new way of attacking Britain carried on until the end of the war in Europe in May 1945.

World War II ended in September 1945. However evacuation did not officially end until March 1946 when it was felt that Britain was no longer under threat from invasion. Surprisingly, even six months after the war ended there were still 5,200 evacuees living in rural areas with their host families.

Most evacuees kept in touch with their hosts long after the war ended.